Alice He

Illustrated by Emma Randall

Rickety Rocket

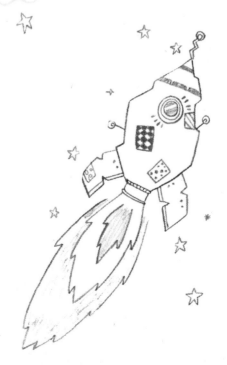

Rickety Rocket

For Nell and Henry

Rickety Rocket
An original concept by author Alice Hemming
© Alice Hemming

Illustrations by Emma Randall
Represented by Plum Pudding Illustration
www.plumpuddingillustration.com

Published by MAVERICK ARTS PUBLISHING LTD
Studio 3a, City Business Centre, 6 Brighton Road,
Horsham, West Sussex, RH13 5BB
+44 (0) 1403 256941
© Maverick Arts Publishing Limited October 2016

A CIP catalogue record for this book is available
at the British Library.

ISBN: 978-1-84886-230-2

Printed and bound in Great Britain by
Marston Book Services Ltd, Oxfordshire

Contents

The Friends

Spacey Stacey

She may spend her days working in the Space Place Café but Spacey Stacey is always on the lookout for adventure.

She is sporty and speedy and loves a challenge, but her friends always come first.

Timble

Timble is a handy robot. He loves to tinker with engines and find the right tool for the job. If he can't, he will invent it.

He is practical, sensible and a very loyal friend.

The Friends

Zip and Zap

These cheeky twins are always together and even finish each other's sentences. They are excitable, energetic and love their food - especially jelly!

Moondoodle

Artistic and dreamy,
Moondoodle has a creative
mind and a great eye for
colour although she does
have a tendency
to get distracted.

The Rivals

Astro Pete

Astro Pete is clever and good-looking and he knows it! He likes to win at  everything but with Spacey Stacey around he might not always come first.

Jack Boom and Jill Zoom

Jack and Jill come as a pair. You will often find them whispering together in the Space Place.

The Space Place

The Space Place is the best café on Planet Fiveways.

In fact, it is the only café on Planet Fiveways!

Spacey Stacey works there and is an excellent cook.

Five-ways

Picnic
Planet

Five
Ways

Planet
Pop!

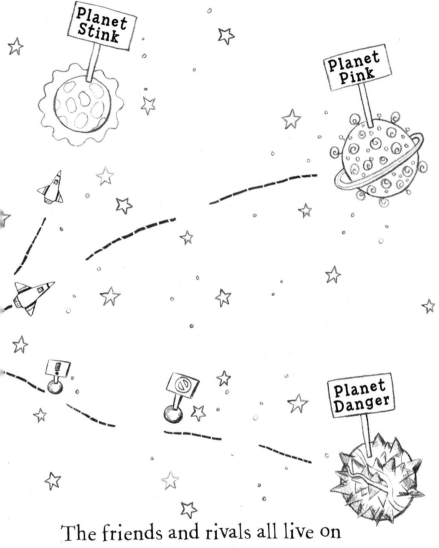

The friends and rivals all live on Planet Fiveways, which is the perfect base for adventures and exploring. It is, as the name suggests, surrounded by five other planets, so there is never any need to be bored.

Rickety Rocket

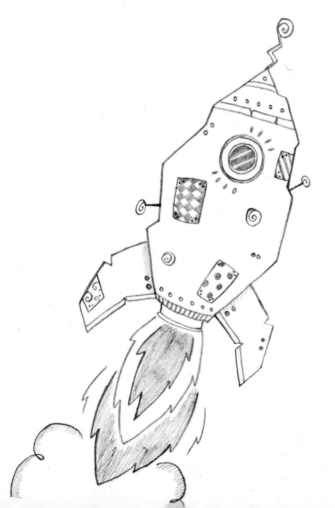

1.

"Look at these beauties," said Stacey, flicking through her latest copy of Space Craft Weekly.

She stood with her best friends in the Space Place café rocket park, jostling to look at the magazine.

"Which one do you like, Stacey?" asked Timble.

"Which colour would you get?" asked Moondoodle. Stacey turned to her favourite page.

"This is the one," she said. "I'd buy this snazzy, purple, sporty rocket and I'd whiz off to Picnic Planet looking super-stylish. For once, I would be the one lazing around rather than serving other people drinks in the Space Place. But – reality check – it's 999.99 space dollars."

Zip and Zap jumped up and down,
pointing to a poster on the wall.

"Why don't you race in the Space Chase
on Saturday?" asked Zip.

"1000 space dollars prize money. If you

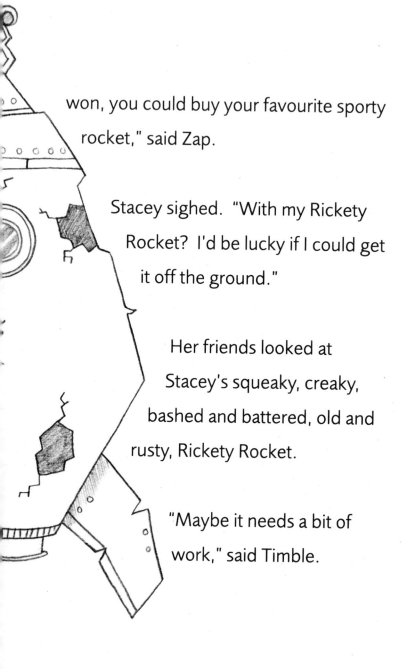

won, you could buy your favourite sporty rocket," said Zap.

Stacey sighed. "With my Rickety Rocket? I'd be lucky if I could get it off the ground."

Her friends looked at Stacey's squeaky, creaky, bashed and battered, old and rusty, Rickety Rocket.

"Maybe it needs a bit of work," said Timble.

"Ha ha, it needs more than a bit of work!" boomed a voice. A tall figure in shiny blue strode past, flashing a white smile.

"Astro Pete," muttered Moondoodle, "He's such a show-off."

Pete read the poster slowly, his smile spreading wider.

"Easy money!" he laughed. "There's nobody out there who can beat me. You should leave the racing to the professionals, Stacey."

He casually booted the Rickety
Rocket and something inside
went

CLUNK!

He strode away, still laughing.

"See?" said Stacey to her friends,
"Everyone would laugh at me."

Timble opened the casing and climbed
inside the rocket with his spanner. After a

couple of minutes of banging and squeaking, his voice echoed out. "The propelling nozzle is still intact," he said.

"In English, please!" said Stacey.

"It means," said Timble, wheeling himself back out from the rocket, "that with a bit of tinkering, the Rickety Rocket could fly in the Space Chase."

"I haven't got time for tinkering," said Stacey, "I have to work in the café all week."

Zip and Zap glanced at each other. Zip looked at Moondoodle. Zap winked at Timble. "We'll help!" they said.

And they did. That week, while Stacey was wiping tables in the Space Place, she hardly saw her friends. Zip and Zap rushed in on Tuesday. "Can we fill up our bucket of water?" asked Zip.

"And have you got any old rags?" said Zap.

Moondoodle dropped by on Wednesday with an old tin of purple paint.

"What do you think of this colour?" she said. And Stacey didn't see Timble at all.

On Friday, Stacey didn't see her friends all day. Jack Boom and Jill Zoom came by for their usual milkshakes. They sat in the corner, whispering. Stacey brought them their drinks.

"Is it true that you're entering the race tomorrow?" said Jack, sniggering.

"It might be," said Stacey. "Is there something funny about that?"

"No, not at all," said Jack, but as Stacey walked back to the counter, she heard their laughter getting louder. Stacey sighed as she cleaned the counter. This was probably all a terrible idea. There was no way she was going to win a race against Jack, Jill and Pete. She would have to tell her friends that the whole thing was off. But just as Stacey was closing up the

Space Place that evening, her four friends

appeared at the door. They looked

paint-splodged and tired but were all

grinning widely.

"Come with us!" they said. "We've got a surprise for you."

They led her round to the rocket park behind the Space Place. A voluminous white sheet covered a familiar-looking shape.

"Ready?" asked Zap.

Stacey nodded.

"Ta-dah!" said Zip and he whipped off the sheet. It was the Rickety Rocket. It looked very different to before.

"Wow," said Stacey. "It's, it's, it's..."

"Purple!" said Moondoodle. "I know it's your favourite colour so I made sure I put it everywhere. I even covered the seats in purple flowery material – look."

"I hammered out the dents in the nose cone," said Timble. "It took ages but it's nearly straight."

"And we scrubbed and cleaned all the windows," said Zip and Zap. "You can see through them now."

"What do you think, Stacey?" asked
Moondoodle.

Stacey looked at the rocket. It was still just
as rickety but now it was a violent shade of
violet – ten times worse than before. If
she raced in this, the whole town would
laugh at her.

Then she looked at the wide-eyed
expectant faces of her friends, who had
worked so hard all week.

"It's perfect," she said.

...

The Great Space Chase!

On the day of the Space Chase, the racers lined up with their spectacular spacecraft. Jack Boom buffed his super speedy GX77. Jill Zoom polished her flashy, fast KP606. Astro Pete patted his shiny shuttle. And Spacey Stacey leaned glumly against the Rickety Rocket as her friends busied themselves around her.

A crackly voice blared out from the loudspeaker.

"All competitors at the ready, the Great Space Chase is about to begin."

"Looks like this is it," said Stacey. "Wish me luck!"

"Don't go too fast," said Zip. "Or too slow," said Zap.

"Keep your eye on Planet Pink," said Timble.

"And take my lucky moon rock," said
Moondoodle.

The four friends raced over to join the
watching crowds and Stacey climbed into
the Rickety Rocket.

"Good luck everyone!" called Stacey to the
other racers.

"You're the one who needs the luck," said
Jack.

"You should stick to serving milkshakes,"
said Jill.

"You'll be looking at my rudder all the way!" said Pete.

Stacey didn't reply. She felt a sudden surge of adrenalin. She pushed her helmet onto her head, fastened her safety belt and gritted her teeth. She was going to finish this race whatever they said.

The voice from the loudspeaker started up again:

"Welcome to the great Space Chase. One thousand space dollars will be awarded to the first person to reach Planet Pink and return to the starting point. Stand by for the countdown..."

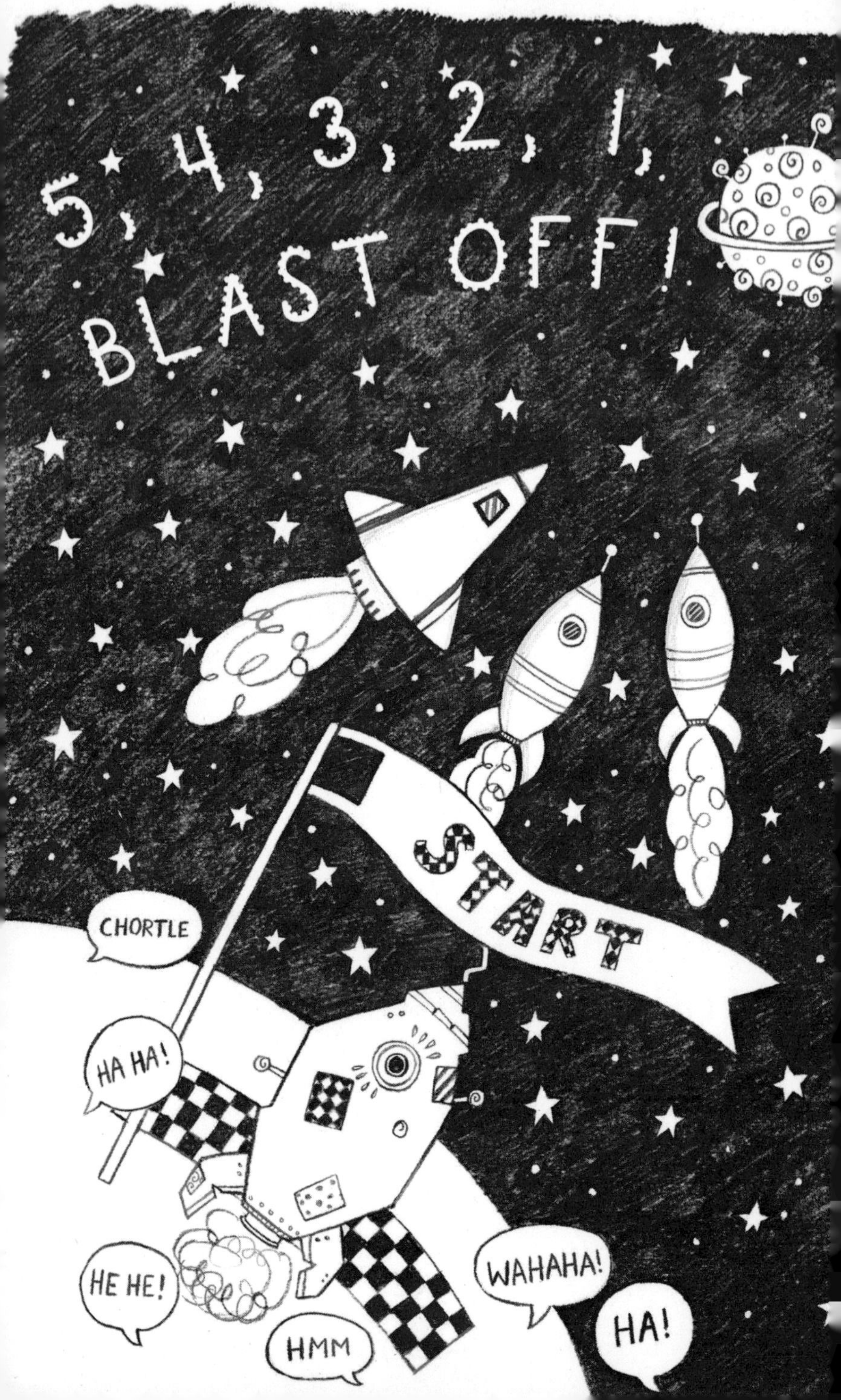
5, 4, 3, 2, 1,
BLAST OFF!
START
CHORTLE
HA HA!
HE HE!
HMM
WAHAHA!
HA!

As soon as the words were spoken, the shiny shuttle shot off into the stars. The GX77 and the KP606 were in close pursuit.

Stacey tried to get the Rickety Rocket to wheeze and creak into action. Eventually it did blast off, and one of its boosters fell to the ground.

SMASH!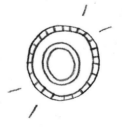

Despite the loud **CHUG, CHUG, CHUG** of

the engine, Stacey was sure she could hear laughter from the crowds below.

Off she chugged, miles behind the others. Astro Pete was leading the way straight to Planet Pink. Jack Boom and Jill Zoom were fighting for second place.

One went right and the other went left. First it was Jack, and then it was Jill. They were so busy looking at each other that they forgot to look where they were going.

"They've taken their eyes off Planet Pink,"

said Stacey, to herself. "They're heading towards Planet Stink."

And it was true: the GX77 and the KP606 disappeared in completely the wrong direction.

Stacey kept a nice straight line. "Not too

fast," she said, "but not too slow. Maybe I
need a bit more power."

The Rickety Rocket heaved and groaned
and part of a wing broke away and
spiralled into space.

CRACK!

SHWWEEEEEEE!

42

Astro Pete zoomed easily around Planet Pink. Stacey watched him heading back as she kept her steady line. As she rattled slowly forwards, she lost a fin, a door and part of the nose cone.

BANG!

CRASH!

SMASH!

"Astro Pete might win but I am going to hold my head up in second place," said Stacey, clutching her lucky moon rock. It looked like an easy victory for Astro Pete but as he hurtled towards the finish line, he looped the loop, waving to the crowds below.

"Look where you're going, Pete!" shouted Stacey, but of course he couldn't hear her.

And he couldn't see the large globe of
rock heading in his direction.

"An asteroid!"

KABOOM!

The shiny shuttle exploded in a glittering firework display.

Luckily Astro Pete pressed the eject button just in time. He parachuted to safety with a face as long as the shiny shuttle had been.

Somehow, Spacey Stacey kept on going. She made a slow circle around the beautiful gas rings of Planet Pink and spluttered back in the direction she had come from.

CHUG CHUG CHUG CHUG CHUG

There wasn't much left of the Rickety Rocket but there was enough to get her past the finish line. And this time, as she landed, she definitely heard the crowds. Four familiar faces were the first ones to come and congratulate her.

HOORAY!

"What will you buy with the prize money, Stacey?" asked Timble.

"Something fast?" said Zip.

"Something shiny?" said Zap.
"Something that will make everyone go WOW?" asked Moondoodle.

"You'll see," said Stacey.

...

The following weekend, Stacey took the four friends back to the rocket park to see her new purchase.

"Ta-dah!" she said and Zip, Zap, Timble and Moondoodle were very surprised to see...

A SQUEAKY, CREAKY, BASHED AND BATTERED, OLD AND RUSTY, RICKETY SPACE BUS.

"It's not snazzy," said Zip.

"Or sporty," said Zap.

"Or speedy," said Timble.

"It's not even purple!" said Moondoodle.

"I know," said Stacey, "but the most important thing is that it has enough room for all my friends. Now, who wants to go to Picnic Planet?"

Jetpack
Jelly

Jelly filled The Space Place.   Red and orange jelly quivered on the counters, purple jelly jiggled on the shelves and individual stripy jellies filled the tables.

Stacey was jostling a bright yellow jelly from its mould, when Zip, Zap and Moondoodle turned up for their usual

Friday treat.

"Welcome to my wibbly, wobbly world,"
said Stacey.

"Wow," said Moondoodle, "Well wobbly.
Why is there so much jelly?"

Stacey put the plate down on a spare
table. "Everyone seems to like it. I made
the first one on Monday and people loved
it. Try some?"

"Mmmm," said Zip, swallowing a spoonful,
"Jellicious!"

"Best jelly ever," agreed Zap.

Stacey smiled. "Only problem is, everyone wants some. People have ordered jelly for weddings, jelly for parties, even jelly for breakfast. I have to deliver all this by the end of the day or I'll be working at the weekend."

"The weekend?" cried Zip.

"We're supposed to be going to Picnic Planet this weekend," said Zap, miserably.

"I know," said Stacey. "I'm trying my best.

Timble has been helping. He made me a hoverboard on Wednesday but I couldn't balance on it with all the jelly. He fitted rocket boosters to my roller boots yesterday but they were no good on the stairs. He says he's got something even better to show me today."

The door opened. "Talking about me?" Timble grinned and staggered in with a large brown box. He put it on the floor. "This is the answer to your wobbly problem."

Stacey opened the box. "A jetpack! Er,

Timble, I've never used one of these
before."

"It's quite simple," said
Timble, "you just put your
arms through like this,
buckle it here, and
press the green
button. You shouldn't
have any problems
steering – it's like
piloting a mini-
rocket."

"What's this red button for?"

"Don't worry about the red button. It
should only be pressed in an absolute
emergency."

"Ooh, what would happen?"

"Just don't worry
about the red
button. You
shouldn't have to
use it."

"Ok," said
Stacey. "Would
you mind

watching the café for me, Moondoodle?
Then I can make a start on these
deliveries."

"Of course," said Moondoodle, "Let me
help you box up all this jelly."

In just a few minutes, Stacey had jetted
through the door with a delivery bag
packed full of plastic boxes.

"This is going to make life much easier,"
said Stacey, shifting the bag as she flew.
She arrived at her first destination: a tall
tower block stretching towards the stars.

"Helix Heights," read Stacey from the sign on the door, "this is the one. Now I could take the boring old lift but I know a quicker way."

Stacey pressed the green button.

WHOOSH!

She jetted up the outside of the building, heading to the

ZOOOOOM!

top floor of Helix Heights.

"This is the way to travel." Stacey crossed her legs and relaxed as she whizzed past each floor.

"Top floor already," she said, hovering by the uppermost window.

She knocked and called, "Jetpack Jelly from The Space Place!"

An excited face appeared from behind a curtain and opened the window.

"Wonderful – my grandchildren will be thrilled," she said, taking one box of jelly and handing Stacey a silver coin in thanks.

"Glad to be of help," called Stacey as the lady closed the window.

"This is so easy! I am going to have these delivered by lunchtime and be ready for Picnic Planet tomorrow."

Stacey patted herself on the back and danced a mid-air jetpack jig. She punched the sky with both fists, somersaulted forwards, flipped backward and began her descent. But at floor forty-three she heard

an unexpected

THWANG!

Stacey had stopped. The jetpack was still
whirring but she seemed stuck in mid-air.
She looked around and saw her problem –
three pairs of spotty pants, five odd socks

and a well-worn T-shirt.

She was caught on a washing line. She pressed the green button but the line was wedged under her jetpack. She attempted another somersault but got even more tangled and nearly ended up with the pants on her head.

'This is bad,' she said to herself as she swayed, legs dangling over nothing.

She looked down. The ground was a long, long way off, so there was no way she could remove the jetpack. A pipe jutted out of the wall just below but she wasn't going to risk the jump. Music blared out from the building. Stacey twisted herself around and peered through the window. She could just about see a figure dancing. He was shaking maracas and moving snake-like hips to the beat.

"Help!" she cried, "I'm stuck!"

The figure shimmied backwards, pink sequinned jacket flashing.

"Help!" called Stacey, louder this time, and banged carefully on the glass, trying not to upset her balance.

As the figure twirled, Stacey instantly recognised the face, despite the rose between his teeth.

"Astro Pete!"

Astro Pete dropped the flower. He drew closer to the window, fiddling nervously with his maracas, his red face clashing with his pink jacket.

The lively music rang out even louder as Pete opened the window.

"Spacey Stacey! You've rather caught me by surprise. I was just doing some housework," he mumbled, "and I was trying to decide where to put these maracas..."

"Look," said Stacey, "I really don't care what you get up to when you're at home. But I'm a bit stuck here. It's a long story, involving jelly deliveries. If you can help get me down I promise never to mention your dancing to anyone, ok?"

"Ok," said Pete, climbing onto the windowsill and inching his way towards Stacey.

"Take my hand," he said, stretching towards her. But Pete's shiny trousers were not made for crawling along windowsills and just as Stacey grabbed his hand, Pete slipped.

"Aaargh!" called Pete, his flailing arms grabbing at the air. Fortunately he landed with both feet on the pipe below.

Stacey bent forwards, keeping tightly hold

of Pete's hand as he tried to keep his balance on the pipe.

"What are we going to do now?"

"Can't that thing get us out of here?" asked Pete, pointing to the jetpack.

Stacey shook her head. "I keep pressing the green button but it doesn't do a thing – look."

Stacey pressed the green button and the jetpack whirred and spluttered but remained firmly trapped.

"What about the red button?" called Pete.

"Timble said never to use the red button – only in an absolute emergency."

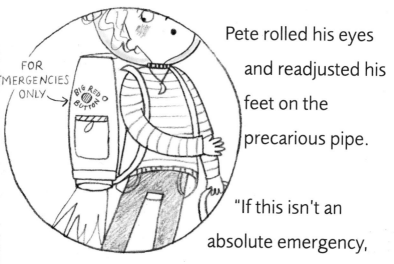

FOR EMERGENCIES ONLY →

BIG RED BUTTON

Pete rolled his eyes and readjusted his feet on the precarious pipe.

"If this isn't an absolute emergency, then I don't know what is. Press the red button!"

Spacey Stacey took a deep breath and pressed the red button. Nothing happened. Pete and Stacey exchanged a nervous glance.

A slow juddering began deep within the jet pack.

JUDUDUDUDDUUDDUDUDUUDD

The juddering became a rumble.
RUMBLE RUMBLE RUMBLE RUMBLE

and then
BANG, BANG, BANG!

WHEEEEEEEEE!

With a sudden explosion, Stacey jolted
forwards, pulling the washing line from
the wall. She dropped for just long
enough for

Pete to grab
her around the waist and then, the jetpack
shot out a super-powerful jet. Spacey
Stacey and Astro Pete rocketed high into

the air,

past the roof of Helix

Heights, past a roaming

satellite and towards the bright stars

above them.

"AAAAAAARGH!" called Astro Pete.
Stacey tried moving left and then right but
it didn't work.

"I can't control it!"

"If we keep heading this way, we'll crash on Planet Stink!" But something else was happening deep within the jetpack

KHUKHUKUKU... **POOOF!**

A hatch opened and a giant colourful cloth billowed out from the jetpack, attached to dozens of fine lines. It widened in the sky above them and caught a breeze.

"Good old Timble!" laughed Stacey. "He thinks of everything. Now we can paraglide back!"

Astro Pete raised his hand in a high five but thought better of it and quickly clung back around Stacey's waist.

The journey back was much smoother than the journey there. Stacey gained control of the wing and steered them safely along.

From up in the clouds they could see clusters of buildings and the tops of trees. The washing line was still attached and fluttered out behind them like a tail, socks and pants fluttering and flapping.

"I liked your dancing back there, in the flat," said Stacey. "I know you don't want me to talk about it but I thought you were really good."

"My Mum taught me when I was little." said Pete. "I used to win competitions before I got into space racing."

"You shouldn't hide it, then. It should be something to be proud of..." said Stacey, but Pete had stopped listening and was looking past the buildings to the streets below.

"Oh no," said Pete, "I can see a whole crowd of people. Even Jack Boom and Jill Zoom."

"Is that Timble and Moondoodle? And Zip and Zap?" cried Stacey, "Here, hold this jelly and I'll give them a wave."

But Pete was trying to shrug off his sparkly jacket. He failed to catch the bag of jelly boxes, which plummeted below them. The lids fell away and red, orange and purple jellies tumbled slowly down, like half-deflated balloons, breaking into wobbly pieces as they fell.

"I can't watch!" said Stacey, closing her eyes.

"We'll be chased by a furious jelly-spattered mob!" moaned Astro Pete.

But the crowd below didn't look furious. Stacey could hear laughing. Several people were staggering backwards with their mouths open. One particularly inventive type had turned his umbrella upside down to catch as much as he could.

Spacey Stacey and Astro Pete landed safely on the ground to happy cheers.

...

Later, back at the Space Place, Stacey was once again boxing up jelly in the kitchen. "I should still be able to get them all delivered in time thanks to your forward-thinking, Moondoodle."

"It was nothing," said Moondoodle. "It was such a quiet afternoon in here I thought I might as well carry on making jelly."

"Perfect. There's just enough for this afternoon. I'll need more for next week, though. I've had loads of orders for this afternoon - everyone thought it was a publicity stunt," said Stacey.

"We half thought so too, when we saw Astro Pete in his snazzy costume." said Timble. "In fact, if it wasn't planned, why on earth was he dressed like that?" Stacey pretended not to hear. She had promised to keep quiet, even though she had been the one doing the rescuing in the end.

"It has all worked out perfectly: seventeen more jelly orders for next week and there's still time to go to Picnic Planet. Which jelly shall we take with us? Zip and Zap, you can choose."

Zip and Zap held hands and spun around in a circle.

"Yum – let's have a bit of everything! Hooray for Picnic Planet! And hooray for jetpack jelly!"

Picnic
Planet

"Picnic Planet here we come!" Spacey
Stacey piloted the space bus skillfully
through the stars. The smell of freshly
baked bread drifted through from the
hamper on the back seat, where her four
friends had made themselves comfortable.

Zip and Zap lifted the lid to take a peek at

all the goodies inside. Nestled in the middle, in a square box, was a giant, orange carrot jelly from the Space Place.

"Mmmm," said Zip, lifting the lid at the corner.

"No nibbling until we get there," ordered Timble.

"But it looks so good," said Zap.

"It's ok," said Moondoodle, "we're nearly there – look!" They drew nearer and nearer to Picnic Planet.

"Perfect weather," said Stacey, expertly parking the space bus.

They piled out into the car park and gazed around. The sky was clear, the grass was blue and all three suns blazed above them.

"Where is everyone?" asked Timble, puzzled. "Picnic Planet is normally packed on a beautiful day like this."

"Maybe the space bunnies put people off," said Moondoodle, pointing to the signs, "Look: 'Warning: Space Bunnies' and 'Do not feed.'"

"Bunnies!" laughed Zip, "Who'd be scared of a bunch of bunnies?"

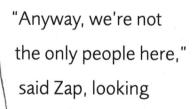

"Anyway, we're not the only people here," said Zap, looking

over to the other side of the car park, where three familiar spacecraft were landing.

"Oh no, it's Astro Pete and co," said Timble.

"Be nice," said Stacey. She waved and smiled. Pete reluctantly waved back while Jack Boom and Jill Zoom sniggered to each other.

"Would you like to join us?" shouted Stacey.

"No thanks," said Pete.

"No way," said Jill. "Our chocolate cake is too good to share."

"Phew," said Timble, and set off to find a picnic spot on the other side of the field.

"Look at the way the suns are sparkling on those treetops," said Moondoodle, half-closing her eyes, "I'm going to take my watercolours to the top of the slope and paint a quick study."

"What about the food?" said Zip and Zap.

"You guys set it all up, I'll only be a couple of minutes," said Moondoodle.

Stacey put up a purple parasol and they spread the red checked picnic blanket beneath it. They opened the hamper and laid out

93

the tasty treats on colourful plates. As well as the giant jelly, they had fresh bread, Starmite sandwiches, crunchy vegetable sticks, spaceman pie, pizza pizzazz and fizzy pop. They each had a comfy cushion, a star sprinkled napkin and plastic knives and forks.

"You've thought of everything," said Timble. "This looks like a proper feast."

"If Moondoodle isn't quick, there won't be anything left," said Zip, grabbing a handful of crisps.

"We'll call her back," said Stacey, "Hang on a minute, who's this little fellow?"

A fluffy silver rabbit with floppy ears lolloped towards them, nose twitching curiously. He stopped a couple of metres away from the picnic blanket.

"Hello," said Stacey, "you're a cute little thing. Here, have a carrot."

The rabbit hopped cautiously towards them, took the carrot and nibbled shyly, keeping his distance.

"Erm, the signs say not to feed the space bunnies," pointed out Timble.

"Does he look dangerous to you?" asked Stacey, laughing. He hopped nearer and she scratched him gently between the ears. "What do you think he's going to do – attack us?"

The bunny seemed to understand and leant back on his hind legs with wide, innocent eyes.

Zip and Zap both laughed but stopped abruptly when, without warning, the bunny took a giant leap forward.

BOING!

He grabbed the plate of jelly in his front paws.

"Huh?" said Stacey.

"No!" cried Zip and Zap.

"Stop him!" shouted Timble, making a swipe for the long-eared bandit.

Stacey jumped to her feet and tried to seize the rabbit, but he was too quick for her. He threw the jelly to a waiting friend, darted around her legs and disappeared into the bushes. They all chased after the second bunny and Zip and Zap even lay on their tummies to get a better look but he had vanished.

"Well!" said Stacey, "I had been looking forward to a bowl of jelly."

"Me too," said Zip.

"And me," said Zap, "Oh well, let's get stuck in to the other food."

They headed back to the picnic but as they emerged from the bushes, Timble put his hands to his head in horror.

"The blanket!" he cried, "Quick!"

Silver space bunnies of all sizes

surrounded the picnic blanket.
There was a bunny at each corner
and bunnies lined along each
edge.

As the first
bunny picked up the
blanket in his mouth, it was
clear what they meant to do. And
Stacey, Timble and Zip and Zap were too
far away to stop them.

The space bunnies lifted the blanket clear
off the ground, complete with plates,

napkins, Starmite sandwiches and every last carrot stick.

By the time the friends were back by the hamper, all they could see were twenty white bobtails disappearing over the hill. Tinny space bunny laughter echoed all around.

"Anything left in the hamper?" asked Timble.

"Nothing," said Stacey, turning it upside down, "Every crumb of our lunch was on that picnic blanket. I'm so sorry, everyone. There's only one thing for it."

She strode over to Astro Pete, Jack Boom and Jill Zoom, who hadn't yet sat down for their picnic. It was all packed away in their stylish orange cool box and they were halfway through a game of Frisbee.

"I don't suppose you guys have any food to share?" she asked. "Our entire lunch has just been stolen by space bunnies."

"Space bunnies!" laughed Jack, sticking out his front teeth and waggling his fingers above his head.

"You should have read the warnings," said Jill, pointing in the direction of the signs.

"Oh dear, oh dear," said Astro Pete, smirking. He twirled the Frisbee on his forefinger. "I'm sure we must have something for you." He threw the Frisbee to Jill, who missed it, and opened up their cool box. Stacey's mouth watered at the sight of cheese rolls, crisps and a rich brown, chocolate cake.

"Here you go," said Pete, rummaging in the box and producing a small, plastic-wrapped bundle, "Don't eat it all at once."

"Thanks," said Stacey unenthusiastically and trudged back to her friends with Jack and Jill's usual laughter following her.

At the picnic spot she unwrapped the bundle.

"Celery?" said Zip, "Is that it?"

"This isn't going to fill my rumbly tummy," said Zap, crunching on a stick.

Timble sighed. "We'd better head home," he said. "Let's go and tell Moondoodle."

They climbed up the hill, Stacey and Timble up ahead, Zip and Zap dragging their feet behind.

"It is beautiful," said Stacey, taking in the wide-open space, wispy trees and butterflies. "I can see why Moondoodle wanted to paint up here."

"It would have been a perfect day," said Timble. "What a shame. Oh well, at least it can't get any worse."

"Let's call her," said Stacey. "Moondoodle!"

"MOOOOONDOOOODLE!" they all called.

"MOOOONDOOOODLE!"

"MOOOONDOOOOOOAAAAARGH!" Stacey was so busy looking around her that she forgot to look at her feet. Something gave way beneath her and with a

SLIP, WHEEEEEEE,

BUMP!

Stacey suddenly found herself in a very dark place.

"What happened?" she said, brushing herself down. "Anyone there?"

"We fell down a hole," said Timble's voice beside her. "Hang on a minute." He fumbled for a moment and then a bright light flooded the small space. "I always carry an emergency torch," he explained.

He shone the light around them and saw that they were in a hole in the ground about the size of a garden shed. They looked up. The hole looked a long way off – too far to climb out. A pair of legs dangled above them.

"Is that you, Zap?" called Stacey.

"Yes," replied Zap, "We're going to rescue you. Hold on to my legs."

"Are you sure?" asked Stacey, gingerly pulling on a foot.

"Yes," said Zap. "Zip's got my arms." Stacey held onto Zap's legs and swung for a few seconds.

"Hang on a minute," said Timble, "What's Zip holding on to?"

A faraway voice came from outside: "A branch."

And then,

SNAP,

AAAAAAAAAAARGH!

BUMP,

BUMP,

BUMP.

Zip and Zap fell into the hole, on top of an unimpressed Stacey.

"Great," said Zip. "Now we're all down here. How are we going to get out?"

Timble flashed his torch into every corner of the small space. "There's a little door here," he said, shining the light to the left.

Stacey rattled it.

"Locked."

"What are these little silver balls?" asked Zip, pointing to a heap by the door.

"Ooh," said Zap, "Sweeties! Let me try one."

Stacey grabbed his hand just before Zap popped it into his mouth. "Stop! That looks like space bunny poo to me."

"Yuck!" said Zap, dropping his find.

Timble put his head in his hands. "Great, just as I said things couldn't get any worse, we end up in a space bunny toilet."

"There must be a way out," said Stacey. "Come on, think, everyone!"

So they thought.

"It's no good," said Zap, "I'm too hungry to think. And that rattling door is putting me off. Can you stop it please, Stacey?"

Stacey stood up suddenly. "It's not me! The rattling must be coming from the other side. It must be a bunny. Stand back everyone – I'm going to catch one of those space bunnies and find a way out of here."

She stood beside the doorframe ready to catch a bunny as they came in. The door handle rattled from the other side, the door swung open, and Stacey pounced and grabbed.

"Come here, you pesky bunny!" she yelled, pinning it to the ground.

"Aargh!" said the bunny, in an unbunny-like voice and then, "I'm not a pesky bunny; I'm Moondoodle!"

Stacey let go and sat up.

"Moondoodle!"
cried
everyone,
"How did
you find us?"

"Well, I had just started my painting, when
I saw an amazing sight.   About twenty
silver rabbits all hopping together towards
the horizon. They were so beautiful – they
looked like waves rippling on a shore."

"I wouldn't call them beautiful – more like
annoying," said Timble.

"Anyway, they were carrying something –
I couldn't see what – and I thought what a
lovely sketch I could draw if I could get
close enough. They darted into a burrow
and I climbed in behind them. I followed
the tunnels deeper and deeper until I
ended up here."

"And do you think you'll be able to find
the way out again?" asked Stacey.

Moondoodle smiled. "Of course. But you
might be interested in taking a look in the
room next door, first."

Stacey, Timble, Zip and Zap all squeezed through the doorway into the next room, which was lined from floor to ceiling with shelves.

The shelves were stacked with bottles of pop, fresh fruit, packets of biscuits and well-stocked hampers.

"Those naughty bunnies!" said Stacey, "They must have been pinching people's picnics for weeks."

"Here's our blanket," cried Zip and Zap together.

"I recognise this one too," said Timble, pointing to a stylish orange cool box. "Looks as though the bunnies might have paid a call to Astro Pete when they were finishing their game of Frisbee."

"Well I don't think we will be able to carry that one as well as ours, do you?" said Stacey, laughing. "Come on, let's go and find a new picnic spot."

This time, the friends didn't leave their picnic unattended and they didn't feed any friendly-looking bunnies. Instead they ate until they were ready to pop.

Zip and Zap lay on their backs with their hands on their full tummies.

"I don't know if I'll fit through the door of the space bus," said Zip.

"And if we do, we'll be too heavy to lift off the ground," said Zap.

"Never mind," said Moondoodle, "We'll just have to stay here all week."

Stacey leapt to her feet. "I'm going to run off some of that food," she said. Come on, who's 'it'?"

Just as she started to chase Zip and Zap,
three sorry-looking figures appeared:
Astro Pete, Jack Boom and Jill Zoom.

"You look worn out," said Timble. "Have
you been playing 'it' as well?"

Pete looked at the ground and murmured

"Space bunnies... stole our lunch."

Jack and Jill said nothing.

"What a shame," said Timble. "We found ours in the end. We've just finished the jelly - it was very tasty."

"But we've got lots of other leftovers," said Stacey, making room on the blanket. "Anyone for a carrot stick?"

THE END